The Town Mouse
and
the Country Mouse

retold and illustrated by

Lorinda Bryan Cauley

G. P. Putnam's Sons   New York

Text and illustrations copyright © 1984 by Lorinda Bryan Cauley
All rights reserved. Published simultaneously in
Canada by General Publishing Co. Limited, Toronto.
Printed in the United States of America.
Library of Congress Cataloging in Publication Data
Cauley, Lorinda Bryan.
The town mouse and the country mouse.
Summary: A town mouse and a country mouse exchange
visits and discover each is suited to his own home.
[1. Fables. 2. Mice—Fiction] I. Title.
PZ8.2.C37To   1984   398.2′45293233   [E]   84-11532
ISBN 0-399-21123-3
ISBN 0-399-21126-8 (pbk.)
First paperback edition published in 1984.
First impression.

For my son Mackenzie, with love

The Country Mouse lived by himself in a snug little hole in an old log in a field of wild flowers.

One day he decided to invite his cousin the Town Mouse for a visit, and he sent him a letter.

When his cousin arrived, the Country Mouse could hardly wait to show him around. They went for a walk, and on the way they gathered a basket of acorns.

They picked some wild wheat stalks.

They stopped by the river and sat on the bank, cooling their feet.

And on the way home for supper, they picked some wild flowers for the house.

The Country Mouse settled his cousin in an easy chair with a cup of fresh mint tea and then went about preparing the best country supper he had to offer.

He made a delicious soup of barley and corn.

He simmered a root stew seasoned with thyme.

Then he made a rich nutcake for dessert, which he would serve hot from the oven.

The Town Mouse watched in amazement. He had never seen anyone work so hard.

But when they sat down to eat, the Town Mouse only picked and nibbled at the food on his plate. Finally, turning up his long nose, he said, "I cannot understand, Cousin, how you can work so hard and put up with food such as this. Why, you live no better than the ants and work twice as hard."

"It may be simple food," said the Country Mouse, "but there is plenty of it. And there is nothing I enjoy more than gathering everything fresh

from the fields and cooking a hot supper."

"I should die of boredom," the Town Mouse complained. "I never have to work for my supper, and in my life there is hardly ever a dull moment."

"I can't imagine any other life," answered the Country Mouse.

"In that case, dear Cousin, come back to town with me and see what you have been missing."

So, out of curiosity, the Country Mouse agreed to go. Off they went, scampering across fields while avoiding the cows and down a dirt lane,

edged with bright flowers, until at last they reached the cobblestones
leading into town.

The streetlights flickered eerily, and with each horse and carriage that clip-clopped by, the Country Mouse trembled with fear.

At last they reached a row of elegant town houses, their windows glowing in lamplight. "This is where I live," said the Town Mouse. The Country Mouse had to admit that it looked warm and inviting.

They went inside and crept past the ticktock of the grandfather clock in the hall and into the living room. The Town Mouse led his cousin to a small entrance hole behind the wood basket next to the fireplace.

Once inside, the Town Mouse lit a candle and started a fire. The Country Mouse looked around the room. It was so much grander than his little hole in the old log. Why, his cousin's bed was covered with a fine silk handkerchief as a bedspread.

They had been traveling all day, and the Country Mouse was tired and

hungry. So he was surprised when his cousin started to go back through the entrance hole. "Could we have something to eat before you show me around?" he asked timidly.

"But of course," said his cousin. "That is where we are going. To have a feast of a supper."

They went through the living room and into the dining room and there on a large table was the remains of a fine supper. The Country Mouse's eyes were wide with astonishment. He had never seen so much food all at once, nor so many kinds.

"Help yourself," invited the Town Mouse. "Whatever you like is yours for the taking."

The Country Mouse scampered across the starched white linen and stared at the dishes. Creamy puddings, cheeses, biscuits and chocolate candies. Cakes, jellies, fresh fruit and nuts!

It all looked and smelled delicious. He hardly knew where to begin.
He took a sip from a tall, sparkling glass and thought, "This is heaven.
Maybe I have been wrong to have wasted my life in the country."

He had just started nibbling on a piece of strawberry cake when suddenly the dining room doors flew open and two servants came in to clear away the dishes.

The two mice scampered off the table and hid beneath it. When they heard the doors close again, the Town Mouse coaxed his cousin back onto the table to eat what was left.

But they had hardly taken two bites when the doors opened again and a small girl in her nightdress ran in to look for her doll, which had fallen under the table. This time the Town Mouse hid behind the jug of cream and the Country Mouse crouched in terror behind the butter dish. But she didn't see them.

As soon as the girl was gone, the Town Mouse began to eat again. But the Country Mouse stood listening. "Come on," said his cousin. "Relax and enjoy this delicious cheese."

But before the Country Mouse could even taste it, he heard barking and growling outside the door. "Wha-, what's that?" he stammered.

"It is only the dogs of the house," answered the Town Mouse. "Don't worry. They're not allowed in the dining room." And with that, the doors burst open and in bounded two roaring dogs. This time the mice scampered down the side of the table, out of the room, and back to the hole in the living room just in the nick of time.

"Cousin, you may live in luxury here, but I'd rather eat my simple supper in the country than a feast like this in fear for my life. I'm going home right away," said the Country Mouse.

"Yes, I suppose that the hectic life of the town is not for everybody, but it's what makes me happy. If you ever need a little excitement in your life, you can come for another visit," replied his cousin.

"And any time you want a little peace and quiet and healthy food, come and visit me in the country," said the Country Mouse.

Then off he went to his snug little home in the fields, whistling a tune and looking forward to a good book by the fire and a mug of hot barley-corn soup.